YOUR STARS ARE WRONG

YOUR STARS ARE WRONG

Wisdom for the Coming Age of Cthulhu

SAMIR AL-AZRAD

A CTHULHU FOR AMERICA Book

votecthulhu.com

ISBN-13: 978-1721527922
ISBN-10: 1721527923

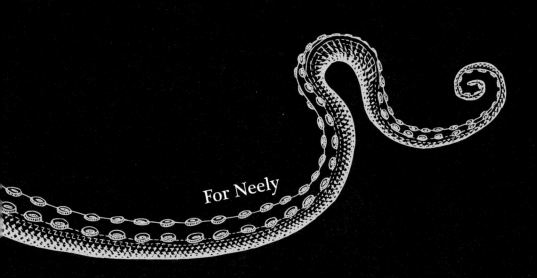

For Neely

"A person who deals in shoggoths should make his pits thrice as deep."

My many-times-great-grandfather would often say that. The wisdom of the foremost philosopher and scientist of his time was so wickedly sharp many branded him mad.

You probably know my 8th century ancestor as Abdul Alhazred. He wrote extensively of scientific concepts far beyond our current understanding. He described philosophies far removed from today's identitarian schisms.

His works were immediately denounced and burned by the establishment. Out of ignorance they labeled it "insanity-inducing heresy." It is not madness to look at the world with clear eyes and an open mind.

The time-honored wisdom he sought to spread originated from man's distant past when we were gifted by the presence of the gods. These were not the gods you know.

We cavorted and wailed in ecstasy under bloody moons for Them. We chanted and offered up the unworthy in accordance with Their cravings.

We howled to Cthulhu, Yig, and Shub Niggurath.

We chanted for Nyarlathotep, Yog-Sothoth, and Azathoth.

And They replied.

Yet as cosmic cycles enveloped the Old Ones, humanity, absent divine direction, wrapped itself in forgetfulness and spun lies about its future. We elevated false gods in our image and blinkered ourselves to the universe, hiding in a deceptive paper womb.

For his dutiful efforts, Abdul and his works were purged from the system, as it were. How dare someone remind people about their place in the world and their subservience to Those Who Dwell Outside! Even in those antiquarian times vapid memes were popular and writ upon the sides of buildings and the propaganda of the powerful were pale replacements for divine commands.

And what of this volume? I wouldn't dare make a comparison to the wrongly forbidden *Al Azif,* for this is a tome meant for popular consumption with memes that will easily devour the human mind.

It my sincerest desire that this mere fraction of my ancestor's distilled wisdom will percolate through society and catalyze a re-evaluation of the misleading pablum on display every #MondayMotivation, #WednesdayWisdom, and #ThursdayThoughts.

So, dear reader, welcome to the Cult of Cthulhu. Soak in the wealth of information within. Soon, you'll be ready to indulge in more potent volumes.

It is time for humanity to remember.

The Old Ones stir — hunger blossoming as they awaken. We must prepare for them with obeisance and pride.

Ready yourself.

Cthulhu is rising.

Samir al-Azrad

Be the reason someone screams today.

The words
we use
open doors
to worlds
They live in.

The greatest
limitation in life
is our weak,
primitive,
mortal shell.

The distance between your dreams and reality is called insanity.

He rises by lifting others into His maw.

PRESERVING

FRIENDSHIP

IS AS EASY

AS BURYING

THEIR CORPSES

IN THE CELLAR.

Exchange your
thought-patterns with
someone else and

your

world will

change.

Reach for a forbidden tome.

It is a weapon.

You don't need a reason to eat people.

You cannot

CONTROL

a mind freed by

MADNESS

The good
die young.

Evil is eternal.

No matter what people think of you, always keep chanting:

"Fhtagn!"

Your perseverance
and hard work

mean nothing

to the cold,
dark cosmos.

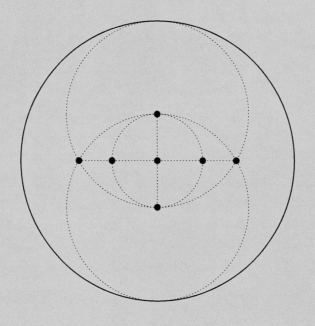

Nothing is more radical than TABOO knowledge.

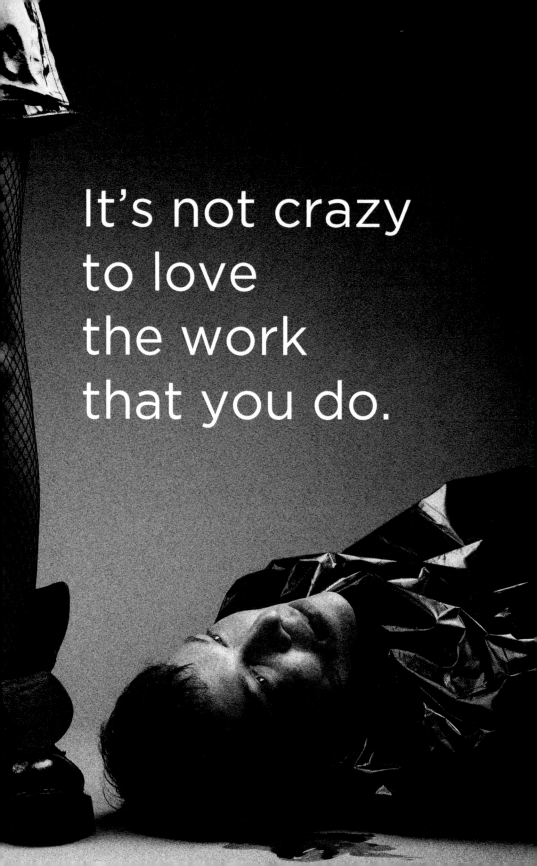

It's not crazy
to love
the work
that you do.

Challenging people are in your life for a reason...

that shoggoth isn't going to feed itself, you know.

Wear gloom like a cloak so that it may feast upon every facet of your pathetic life.

Someday you will look back and see exactly what has been stalking you.

The surest investment you can make is a reservation in the ancestral crypt.

Other worlds are not only possible, they are already here.

On quiet nights
you can hear
them howling.

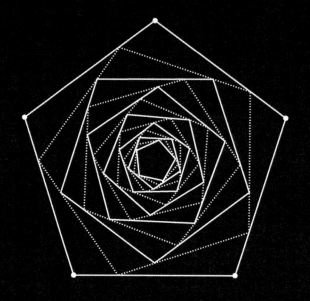

The Universe
is positively
against you.

Nothing has
the power to
radically change
a life more
than death.

Power
concedes

NOTHING

without a spell
of binding.

Things couldn't possibly get worse?

Yes.

Yes they can.

Look for opportunity in every situation to punch holes in the walls of reality.

Don't be pushed around by your problems.

Toss them into a bottomless pit.

Non-Euclidean Pi is the constant of insanity.

Satisfaction is inside every tasty mortal.

If you want
to achieve
greatness

_____

read the
Necronomicon.

Despair thrives
behind the
small hope
of escaping
your downfall.

You are not a star, but an errant cosmic stain.

It is always
more important
to have blood
spilled in your
name than
be loved.

The path of

perseverance

leads to

dark knowledge

you are

incapable

of processing.

Don't just wish.

Chant and sacrifice for it.

The price is worth it.

Your doom is always a work in progress.

Don't look for someone to solve your problems.

Look for something to eat the cause of your problems.

It's only when you faithfully step off the ledge will you realize humans

were

never

meant

to

soar.

Confidence is not
"they will like me."

Confidence is
"I'll carve their
eyes out if
they don't."

If your dreams do not scare you, you haven't even begun to search for Kadath.

The more things don't change,

the more they stay insane.

Extinguishing the light of other people's candles is a great way to collect wax to build a bigger votive candle.

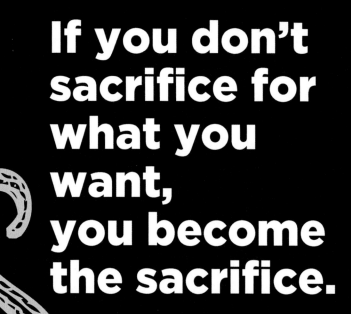

If you don't sacrifice for what you want, you become the sacrifice.

I have a dream
that all humans
are eaten in
equal portions.

Life

shrinks

or

e x p a n d s

**in proportion
to one's ability
to consume
another's
life force.**

Every good thing you
do creates ripples.

**Every evil thing you
do churns waves.**

DO SOMETHING TODAY THAT YOUR FUTURE SELF WILL FOREVER CURSE YOU FOR.

Write your
troubles in
your grimoire.

Carve your
successes
into flesh.

Civilization is a cheap and easy way of domesticating the *homo sapien* parasite.

Your screams will not protect you.

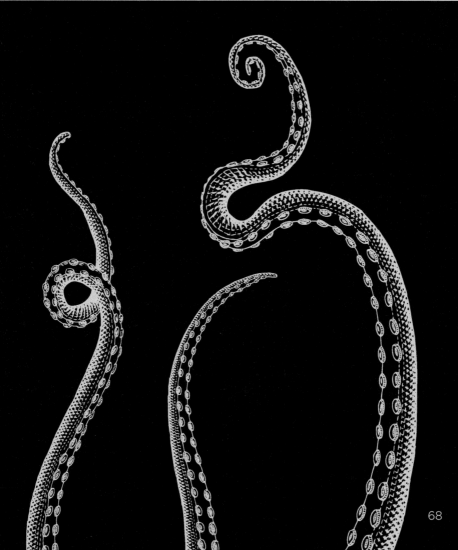

You are,
and have
always been,

supremely
unimportant
to the cosmos.

What consumes your
mind, controls your life,

for you are not you
anymore, but It,

and It is enjoying Itself
very, very, very much.

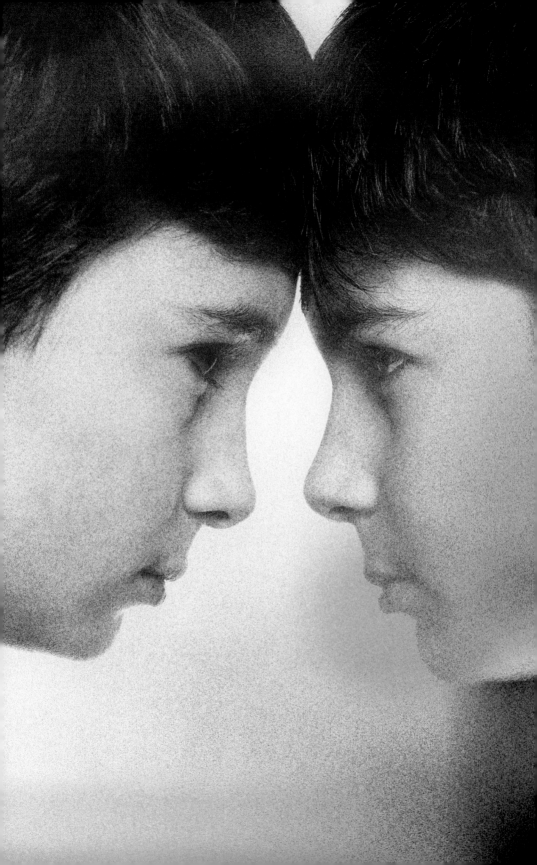

Be fearless
in the
pursuit
of what
you fear.

We're
waiting.

Everything you've ever wanted is on the other side of death.

Don't be pushed by your problems.

Be led by your mania.

Take time to sate the gnawing hole where your soul used to be.

Indulge in a transtextual relationship with a blasphemous tome.

Truly successful people not only want to win,

they will sacrifice everyone to do it.

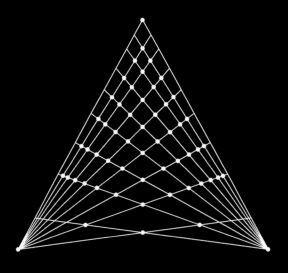

The journey of
a billion parsecs
begins with the
extraction of
your brainstem.

Be brave enough to stand alone before Dread Cthulhu, you'll be easier to scoop up and devour.

It's not what you say out of your mouth that determines your life.

It's what you whisper to the darkness that has the most power.

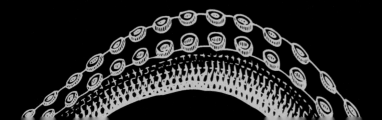

Be merciless to yourself,

then let that pain
flood the world.

Do what you can
to get a head.

Then consume it
for nourishment.

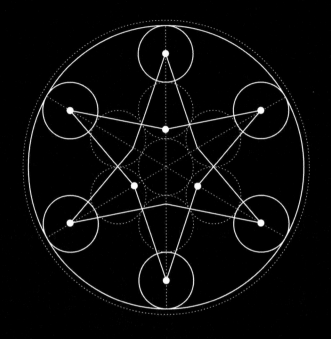

WHERE THERE IS DISCIPLINE,
THERE IS POWER.

WHERE THERE IS POWER,
THERE IS DECADENT DIABOLISM.

There is no elevator to success.

It's in the basement, in the dark, lurking behind the furnace.

Eldritch rites

need

human wrights

and

human wrights

need

eldritch rites.

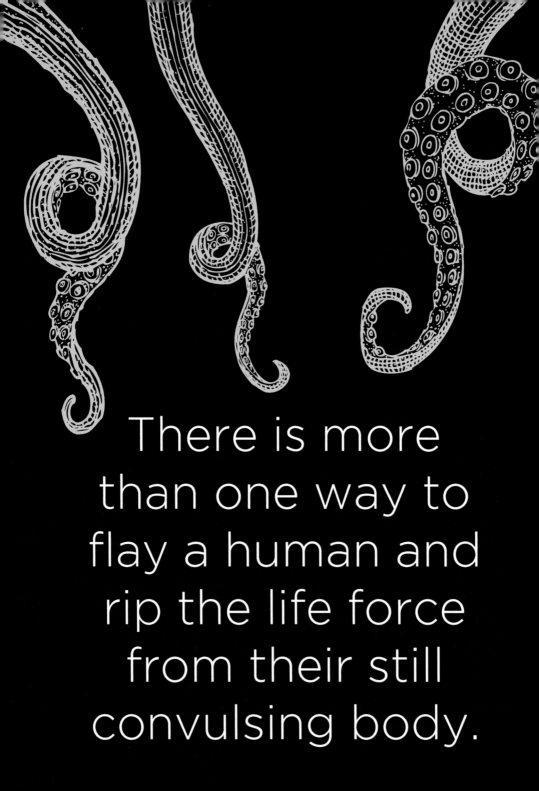

There is more than one way to flay a human and rip the life force from their still convulsing body.

In every moment

for every reason

choose lunacy.

KNOW THAT

DEEP INSIDE,

YOU ARE STILL

A SMALL, INSECURE,

WEAK PRIMATE

UNWORTHY OF EXISTENCE.

Life isn't about finding yourself.

Life is about creating a new you from "donors."

Everything seems impossible until Cthulhu rises from the sea & wipes out civilization.

If you're not making someone else's life a **torment** you're living yours wrong.

A willingness to
break all natural laws
brings true success.

Keep your face always toward the shadows

so as to stare your doom

in what you think is its face.

Eat for the body you want...

   that is growing out of your back.

Throw madness around like blood-caked confetti.

WE HAVE IT IN
OUR POWER TO
REBOOT THE WORLD
INTO SOMETHING
FAR STRANGER.

Be like the Yellow Sign.

Stick in someone's mind until they go stark raving mad.

Never let

a bad cantrip

be the end of a

good summoning.

Wake up and smell the fetid rot.

The world has plenty of whiners...

**but it is
the cultist
who toils
to doom
the planet.**

DO WHAT THEY

BEGGED SHOULD

NEVER BE DONE.

Your life is
falling apart
because entropy
is u n i v e r s a l .

A dream can become reality

simply intone the right sequence of morphemes.

SOMETIMES YOU NEED TO GO OFF THE GRID TO PRACTICE YOUR ABOMINABLE EXPERIMENTS.

The road less
travelled ends
right before you
are rended into
a bloody mist.

Death happens.

Unless you sacrifice someone
for immortality.

IT'S NOT HOW BAD YOU ARE,

IT'S HOW BAD YOU WANT TO BE.

**Don't tell people
your dreams.**

**Unleash your
nightmares
upon them.**

Sticks and stones may break your bones,

but the right sigils will summon revenge.

Sometimes the smallest things can
take control of your nervous system.

The Plateau of Leng is built of the skulls of highly motivated people.

THE TWO MOST IMPORTANT

DAYS IN YOUR LIFE ARE

THE DAY YOU ARE BORN

AND

THE DAY YOU FIND YOUR
ANCESTRAL LINEAGE IS CURSED.

Dominance is not a goal.

It is the by-product of an evil plan well executed.

A willingness to break all natural laws brings true success.

Don't stress about the future. Time is not linear. Cthulhu has already consumed humanity.

Reanimate a life that you can never escape from.

Never doubt that a group of committed, devout people can summon the end of the world.

Dare them to lock you in an asylum.

Use incantations to turn

---

the world inside out.

Hope is a delusion.

WHEN YOU WALK

THE PATH OF DEATH,

DARKNESS, AND

DOOM, YOU ARE ONE

WITH THE COSMOS.

Be strong enough to

accept the changes

forced upon you by your

mutating alien genes.

**Do not let us speak of
Darker Days,
let us rather speak of the
End of Days.**

Work toward a world in which morality is irrelevant.

The darkest

caverns are

within reach

if you

just keep

descending.

Of what use are finite beings to those who are infinite?

DEATH

is humanity's number one killer.

Err in the direction of the weird.

People's

fears

go

on

forever.

The madness
you see is a
reflection
of you.

of you.

reflection

you see is a

The madness

Our original guiding stars are Nug and Yeb.

The test of a civilization is in the way that it prepares for its own demise.

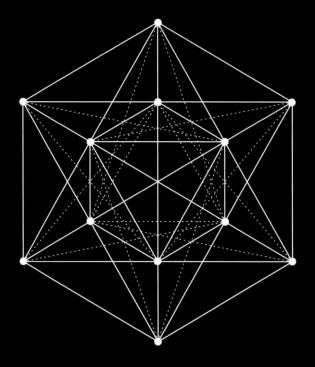

You are never too young to read medieval metaphysics.

Squeeze life
to the fullest
and sup upon
its cruor.

Sorry for the inconvenience.

We are trying to end the world.

Samir al-Azrad has been a fixer, bartender, necromancer, and corporate communications exec. He has survived two plane crashes, explored the Rub'al Khali and completed twenty-six deep dives in the Pacific. He shares his home in Connecticut with his three cats, the ghost of his mother and a growing collection of esoteric (and illegal) tomes. YOUR STARS ARE WRONG is his debut book.

Samir currently serves as Chief Messaging Officer for the Cthulhu for America 2020 campaign. More information can be found at votecthulhu.com.

Made in the USA
Coppell, TX
07 December 2019